Fairy Tale
of Bristol

THE FAIRIES OF BRANDON HILL

TALIE ASHBEE

*To Emily and Annabelle
with love from
Talie* ✶

JELLY BEAN BOOKS · CARDIFF
2021

Fairy Tale of Bristol © Talie Ashbee 2021
Illustrations © Christine Harris 2021
Editor: Shaun Russell
Editorial: Keren Williams

Printed and bound in the UK by
Severn, Bristol Road, Gloucester, GL2 5EU

ISBN: 978-1-913637-77-4

Published by
Jelly Bean Books, Mackintosh House
136 Newport Road, Cardiff, CF24 1DJ
www.candyjarbooks.co.uk

This fairy tale was brought to life with
the help of my three magical children:
Henry Seth, Poppy Isabelle and Tabitha Rose.

Thank you to their wonderful father, Mark, for letting
us chase our dreams, find the fairies and for sharing
this wonderful city with us.

For all the children who stayed brave through the
pandemic. I hope you meet your fairies soon.

Talie

– CHAPTER ONE –

The House with the Yellow Door

Rose sat gazing out of her new bedroom window. She could see trees covered in pretty pink blossom in the park opposite, with squirrels bounding up and down them.

'Mummy, please can we go outside now? We just want to see what the park's like. Please, Mummy, we won't be long.'

Mum stopped opening the large brown box for a moment, and turned to the eager faces looking up at her. 'Okay then,' she said. 'Just for a while, but your brother will need to go with you.'

Hearing his name, Seth poked his head around the door of his bedroom. 'What's the brother got to do now? Are his special powers required? Does he need to stop his crazy little twin sisters getting into trouble yet again?!' He grinned.

Both Isabelle and Rose glared at their older brother, but then ran to him and pleaded, 'Oh, please, Seth, just for a little bit. Mummy is going to be *ages* with all these boxes.'

Hands on her hips, Mum smiled at them. 'It's your stuff as well. I hope you're going to help unpack.'

'We will, Mummy, we will!' they all chorused back.

Mum looked at the boxes stacked up high in the room and gave a big sigh. 'Go on then. Seth, I want you to keep an eye on them. Stick together, okay? You've got half an hour. It should be teatime when you get back.'

'Hooray! Come on, Seth, let's go!' The twins dashed out to find their shoes, while Seth picked up his mobile phone and grabbed his trainers.

As they headed for the door, Mum called out, 'I mean it. Only half an hour. Daddy won't be back until later.'

'Don't worry, Mum, you can trust us,' said Seth.

Mum smiled gratefully. She had to admit that even though she trusted him, it was still hard to let her three babies out of her sight, especially when everything was so new for them. The family had just moved into the house with the yellow door on Brandon Hill, Bristol. It was a big move, leaving their seaside home in Cornwall and relocating to the city, but everyone was excited about their new adventure. Friends and family back in Cornwall couldn't understand the reason for moving to a 'smelly old city', but Mum hoped they had done the right thing. Finding this house by the park and near the children's new schools had seemed like fate. Dad would be able to get more photography work and she really wanted to find a big garden to work in, but for the moment she was going to concentrate on getting the house all sorted and the children settled into school. Everything was going to be fine; she just knew it.

*

Seth, Isabelle and Rose crossed the little road outside the house and went straight into the park. It was incredibly fortunate that their house was so close to a playground. All were keen to explore.

As the children ran up the hill, they spotted a curious little red tower peeking out from behind the trees. 'Look how high it is,' said Rose. 'It goes up into the clouds.'

Isabelle gazed up at the tower on the top of the hill. 'I wonder if you can climb it.'

Seth caught up with the twins. 'Dad says you can, but we can't do it now.'

'Aww!'

'We promised Mum only half an hour. Oh, and I really want to get my computer set up.'

Isabelle rolled her eyes. 'Oh, Seth, you're always on that computer.'

Seth decided not to answer. The girls spotted a sandpit with a slide, and Seth made for a huge climbing frame. Back home he used to go surfing all the time, but he appreciated that Mum and Dad had made this move as much for him as themselves.

'There will be much more to do in the city,' they had said, and so far they had been right.

From the top of the climbing frame he gazed out over the city. The great thing about living on a hill was definitely the view. You could see for miles, right out across the harbour to the hills beyond. You could even see the towers of his school, and the two golden unicorn statues that stood majestically on top of City Hall on College Green.

Through a gap in the Georgian houses, like the one they'd bought, Seth could see the tall masts of the SS Great Britain, and the flags fluttering in the breeze. He wondered what it would have been like to go to sea on a ship like that. He was used to fields and hillsides, and he had been really worried about moving to the city, but as he looked out across the water and saw people in canoes and little boats, he decided maybe it was all going to be okay.

He was jolted out of his thoughts by Rose calling up to him. 'Let's take a quick peek at the tower. We don't have to climb it today, but I just want to take a look, just a little look. It won't take long.'

Seth could never resist her big blue eyes and eager little face. 'Okay then,' he said, with a smile. They clambered up the steep grass slope towards the tower.

'Phew, it didn't look so steep from the house,' said Isabelle.

Seth's mathematical head started to calculate the gradient of the hill. It certainly seemed pretty steep.

Rose found a small pond with stepping-stones and bounced across to climb a tree dangling over it. Isabelle found a little bridge, which looked down onto the pond. Golden fish were darting in and out of the reeds along the edge, and a startled toad jumped into the water with a plop. A gentle cascade of water trickled into the pond, making sparkling ripples across the surface.

'Let's play Pooh-sticks!' exclaimed Isabelle. 'We can drop them over the side of the bridge.'

Further up the hill there were lots of shrubs, and the girls spotted a path leading away from the pond.

'There's bound to be some sticks there, Iz. Come on,' said Rose, pointing.

'Don't go too far, girls!' called Seth. He may be only thirteen but Seth took his responsibility as 'big brother' very seriously, and he was still unsure whether the city was as safe as the countryside. They'd always been told not to talk to strangers, but how on earth did you do that in a city full of people you didn't know? They had to talk to someone!

'It's like a little garden in here, don't you think, Rose?'

'Yes, it's so pretty and I love all these secret paths. I wonder where they all go.'

'Probably to the tower.'

Glossy green shrubs, covered in pretty white flowers, made tall hedges along the path, but every now and then little tunnels could be seen under the bushes.

'I wonder what's in there?' asked Rose. Isabelle got down on her hands and knees, and peered into the bushes.

'Rose, look at this!'

Kneeling down next to Isabelle, Rose could see

several tiny paths going off in different directions.

'What's that sparkling?' asked Isabelle.

Rose inched forward and picked up a pretty, white stone. Holding it up into the sunlight, the pebble glittered like a diamond and both girls gasped with delight. Turning it over in her palm Rose couldn't believe their luck.

'It's beautiful, Iz. Are there any more?'

'Let's have a look,' said Rose, pushing Isabelle out of the way. She carefully crept further along the hidden path.

'Girls, where are you?!' called Seth. He climbed down from the tree and went up the path. *It's nice here*, he thought. There was something calm and peaceful about the garden. It didn't feel like the city at all. There were so many lovely trees.

'Girls!' called Seth again.

Deep in the bushes the girls were too busy to acknowledge Seth, but Isabelle was trying hard to be the sensible one. 'Be careful, Rose, we don't know what's in there. Remember what Daddy always says.'

Rose was far too distracted by a line of shiny pebbles she had found along the path. Unlike the first one, these were not all white; some were sparkly pink, others green, like the sea on a sunny day.

Suddenly, something flashed brightly past her eyes. It was too quick to work out what it was. Isabelle bumped into her bottom. 'Ouch! What's the matter?'

'Shhh. Did you see that?'

'See what?'

'That flash, you must have seen it?' Rose sat back on her heels and Isabelle squeezed in next to her. Another flash, this time just above the girls' heads. Both girls took a sharp intake of breath. Rose exclaimed. 'You must have seen it this time.'

'Yes, I saw. Was it...? Do you think...? Could it really be...?

'FAIRIES!' they both said at once, and grinned at each other.

Seth was peering into the tunnel. 'There you are.

Don't do that. Mum would be really mad if I lost you on the first day!'

Isabelle and Rose stared back at Seth like startled rabbits.

'What've you found?' Seth asked.

Isabelle nudged Rose sharply and shook her head. 'Nothing, Seth, we just found these tracks. Do you think they're made by a rabbit?'

'Probably. Come on, you two, you're getting filthy and Mum will be cross. Also, we've been out for forty minutes, and we promised Mum—'

'Spoilsport,' said Rose, sticking her tongue out.

'We can come back another day.'

Isabelle and Rose scrambled out of the bushes looking glum. As they followed Seth back to the house, they stayed slightly out of earshot. 'Do you really think it was fairies?' whispered Isabelle, smiling.

'Yes, definitely! I just know it, and they live on *our* hillside, right outside our door!' said Rose, her eyes big and round. Isabelle had never seen her quite so excited. 'Let's tell Seth.'

Isabelle paused for a moment. 'No, let's wait. He'll just think we're silly. I think we should come back tomorrow. It can be our little secret for now.'

Rose, her head on one side, thought about it for a moment. 'Okay, just until we know more.'

They smiled at each other, held hands and ran down the hill towards the house with the yellow door where Mum was standing waiting.

CHAPTER TWO

The First Gift

The next morning they started their new school. They were excited but a little bit nervous, even Seth.

'At least my school is not too far away; if there are any problems you can always come next door and get me. I'm sure you'll make some new friends anyway.' Seth wasn't sure who he was trying to convince, himself or the girls. Seth was sometimes a bit jealous of the girls. They had each other, but he often felt left out.

As it transpired, Seth did make some new friends, both musical like him. He knew that Mum had worried about them starting a new school, but she hoped that moving in spring would help. It was Mum's favourite season, and as she said, 'There's always a wonderful sense of hope in the air.'

When they arrived home, Seth settled down to do his homework. Rose and Isabelle could barely contain their excitement when Mum offered to take them up to the park for a run around. They quickly got changed out of their uniforms and were ready to go in minutes.

Mum was impressed. 'Wow, that's the quickest I've ever seen you get changed!' she said. The twins glanced at each other with a secret smile, both knowing exactly where they wanted to go and what they wanted to do.

'Do you think we'll see the fairies again?' whispered Isabelle to Rose when they arrived at the top of the slope.

'Oh, yes, definitely!' Rose was always quite positive.

Mum had a stack of paperwork from the sale of the house with her and Rose watched her head off for a bench to concentrate on them. 'I'll stay here, girls. You go and play, but don't go too far. Once I've finished all this...' She held up the paperwork. '...we can look at the park together.'

'Okay, Mummy. We'll be fine.'

And off they ran, clambering up to the gardens, jumping over the stepping stones and into the bushes where they'd seen the sparkly stones the previous day. 'Do you think they'll be here again, Iz? What if we scared them away?'

Isabelle shook her head, 'I'm sure we didn't. Maybe we should give them a gift, like leaving a tooth for the tooth fairy.' She looked around for something to give the fairies, while Rose tried her pockets.

'Oh, look, I've got that shiny bead I found. Perhaps we can give them that?'

Isabelle took the little bead from her sister's hand and gave it a quick polish with her t-shirt. 'Perfect,' she said. 'I think they'll love that. Let's see what happens.'

Isabelle crawled into the bushes, found the

tunnel, and carefully placed the bead in the centre of the path. The girls then waited.

It was very quiet under the bushes. They could hear birds singing gently above them, and from the pond, the funny croak of a frog. Rose started to fidget. She was getting pins and needles in her feet from sitting still. She looked at Isabelle, who was trying hard not to be distracted, but she was starting to feel a bit uncomfortable too.

'Where are they?' she whispered.

Rose shrugged. 'Maybe they're not here at the moment. They might be gathering flowers to make crowns or twigs to fix their roofs—'

'Or riding mice or making flower perfume,' interjected Isabelle. They both laughed.

Just then they heard Mum calling their names, so they quickly scrambled out of the tunnel and squealed with happiness when they saw Mum, Dad and Seth down by the pond.

Seth was swinging from a tree branch, 'Look who came home early.'

'Daddy!' they both yelled, and ran to give him a

big hug.

'Hello, young ladies, looks like you've been having lots of fun already.' He smiled down at his daughters, taking each by a hand. 'Come on then, let's go and see this tower I've heard so much about.'

'Woohoo!' shouted Seth, jumping down from the tree. 'Race you, girls.' Seth shot up the path. He disappeared up some wide steps as they arrived at the foot of the tower.

Rose looked slightly disappointed. 'Oh! It's not nearly as tall as I thought!' She'd been expecting the tower to start much lower down, but of course they had been looking at it from the bottom of the hill.

'It's almost as if it's had the bottom chopped off!' Isabelle said with a frown. 'Like there's a bit missing.'

They all looked up at the little red tower, with its pretty balconies on the sides and a bigger lookout at the very top. Dad seemed a bit worried. 'Well, it looks plenty tall enough to me. Why don't you all climb up to the top and I'll wait down here.'

Mum glanced at him with a knowing smile.

'You'll be able to wave at Daddy from the top. Come on then!' She led the way through the little door and started climbing the tiny winding staircase.

'Rose, it really is like Rapunzel's tower,' whispered Isabelle. 'It goes up and up and round and round. She'd be able to let her hair down from the top!'

'Yes, you're right, and it's tricky to climb,' Rose puffed.

Seth was last up the stairs and laughed at them both. 'Just wait till we have to go down again! That will be even trickier!'

As they arrived at the first level, they each picked a balcony to look down into the park and out over the city. Mum could see right over to Leigh Woods, across the gorge with its wonderful suspension bridge. She loved that bridge and always felt a tingle of excitement whenever she drove over it, so very high above the River Avon. The first time she had come to Bristol it was all lit up and she'd loved it from then on. In fact, it was probably what made her fall in love with the city.

Seth could see out over to the Wills Tower, with its gothic towers and the university behind. It's where his grandfather used to lecture. He wondered what Bristol must have been like back when Grandad lived there. He knew he'd been in Bristol during the war and Grandad had told him stories of the terrible bombing. Bristol had changed a lot, he remembered him saying, with the old city centre being mainly destroyed.

Seth really liked the buildings that had survived, with their grand doorways and carved stonework, and he loved their new house on Queens Parade. It needed a lot of work doing to it, but Mum and Dad loved that kind of thing, and he knew they'd do a good job. Mum had a pretty little garden, so she was happy. Dad had a cellar that he wanted to turn into a photography dark room. Seth thought it was a bit scary and damp down there, and he wondered what was at the back of the cellar.

Rose and Isabelle picked the front balcony and together stood gazing out at the pretty, coloured houses on the Cliftonwood hillside. They saw the tiny people walking along the waterside in the sunshine and called out to each other as they spotted more and more interesting things.

'Look, Iz, there are the golden unicorns Mummy told us about.'

'Oh, they're so beautiful. I wonder why they're up there. Do you think they flew up and were put under a spell by an evil witch?'

'Maybe, or maybe they're only statues by day and they come alive at night. Wouldn't that be amazing?'

Seth sauntered up behind them and peered over their shoulders. 'Look there's a golden cockerel over on that church too. Maybe they all party together at night.' He rolled his eyes at them and grinned. Seth loved joining in with their fantasy stories. 'I'm going to climb to the very top,' he announced. He went through the other door leading to the top of tower. Rose was about to follow him when something made her stop. She noticed a bright flash down in the park.

'Isabelle, wait!'

Isabelle turned and came back with a questioning

look.

'Look over there, Isabelle.' Rose pointed to the bushes.

Isabelle leaned over the balcony and could see Daddy waving up at them from below. 'Daddy looks so tiny,' she said. As she watched him, she saw another flash, like a crystal catching the light. It was moving in and out of the bushes just behind Daddy.

'Can you see it?' asked Rose. Isabelle nodded and smiled. Without a word they both darted back through the door to the stairs, calling to Mum that they were going down, before carefully following the spiral with its tiny steps all the way down, and dashing out into the sunlight.

'Hey, girls, what's got you in such a rush? What did you see up there?'

'Nothing, Daddy!' they both shouted.

Dad was standing by a plaque he had found. 'Hang on, girls. Have you seen this?'

The girls were impatient to see whatever was sparkling, but quickly took a look at the plaque to keep their dad happy.

It said the tower was called Cabot Tower, after an Italian explorer from Venice called John. Dad read the plaque out loud:

'This tower was erected by public subscription in the 61st year of the reign of Queen Victoria to commemorate the fourth centenary of the discovery of the continent of North America, on June 24, 1497, by John Cabot. Who sailed from this port in the Bristol ship Matthew, with a Bristol crew.'

'And,' he continued, 'You can see a replica of the Matthew ship down in the harbour. Maybe we could take a trip on it one day if you'd like? I know how much you two like exploring!'

Despite being interested, the girls were eager to get on. 'That would be brilliant, Daddy, but can we do a bit of exploring ourselves, just down in the gardens?'

Dad smiled and shooed them off. 'Just for a bit, and then I'd like to see how your new bedrooms are coming along.'

'Okay,' they said together and ran off down the path to the tunnel in the bushes.

They stopped just at the entrance and peeped in, neither speaking. Wide-eyed, Rose looked at Isabelle and then back at the tunnel. There on the little path where they'd left their gift lay two beautiful pink rosebuds, each sitting on a perfect round green leaf.

– CHAPTER THREE –
New Friends

Without a word, Rose and Isabelle crept into the tunnel. They each picked up a tiny flower bud. Huge grins on both their faces, they looked at each other before staring into the depths of the bushes, desperately trying to seek out their new friends.

'Thank you, fairies,' whispered Rose. 'These are very beautiful.' Rose looked at Isabelle, hoping she'd be able to coax them out.

'We'd love to be your friends,' Isabelle said shyly. 'Your garden is very pretty and we promise we will take care of it.'

The girls were silent and still, hardly daring to

breathe in case they broke the spell. Everything had gone very quiet as if the whole of Bristol had suddenly been frozen in time. There wasn't a sound: no birds, no people, not even the wind in the trees. It was as if a magical veil had fallen over the girls, sitting quietly holding their perfect flower buds in the palm of their hands.

Isabelle and Rose both took a deep breath and the veil lifted. As birdsong began and leaves on the trees rustled once more, a tiny shimmering figure fluttered down from above them and landed in front of the twins.

'Hello,' said the fairy.

'Oh, goodness me. Hello, little fairy!' Isabelle's face lit up with happiness.

'Hello! It's so lovely to meet you at last,' said Rose, bending down to get closer.

The fairy was no taller than a robin. She had bouncy blonde curls and was wearing the most delicate, pale green dress dotted with silver raindrops. Rose noticed that the fairy was wearing the most beautiful, green velvet slippers – the same emerald shade as her eyes. Her dress danced around her, lighter than a breeze, and her wings shimmered with every movement. The twins had never seen anything so perfectly beautiful in their lives.

'I'm Dewdrop,' she said in a tinkling voice, rising gracefully up into the air to be eye-level with the girls. Rose was still staring, open-mouthed at the exquisite creature, so Isabelle answered for them both.

'My name is Isabelle and this is my twin sister Rose. We've just moved into the house at the bottom of the hill.'

'The one with the yellow door,' said Rose, wanting to join in at last.

Dewdrop smiled and did a twirl of happiness. 'Oh, that's wonderful. You'll be able to come and see us. I'd love for you to meet some of my friends here on the hillside. We don't play with children much anymore. They just don't seem to come outside very often.'

Isabelle laughed. 'Oh, that sounds like our brother, Seth. He's always playing games on his computer, although he does have some with elves and dwarves in them. I'm sure he'd love to meet you.'

'Oh no, let's keep Dewdrop to ourselves for a little while,' said Isabelle.

Dewdrop giggled. 'Would you like to see our home?'

'Oh, yes please!' chorused the girls excitedly.

Just then they heard Dad's voice calling to them. 'Come out, come out wherever you are. Girls!'

'Oh no, we've got to go.' Rose was very disappointed.

Dewdrop floated down and sat on her knee. 'Don't worry, only children can see us. When people grow up they lose their fairy sight. Sometimes they do see us out of the corner of their eye, but their minds have become so clouded with worry and responsibility. It's quite sad really. Why don't you come back tomorrow and I will show you our home?'

Rose and Isabelle both clapped their hands. 'Yes please!' As they crawled quickly back out of the tunnel, Rose called back, 'See you tomorrow.'

Just as they emerged onto the path, Dad came around the corner. 'Ah, there you are, little rascals, what on earth were you doing in there?' he said.

Isabelle and Rose looked at each other with a mixture of panic and excitement. 'Looking for rabbits, Daddy,' said Rose, with a sweet smile.

Dad laughed. 'Come on then, let's get back to our new home and you can give me the grand tour.'

Taking each of them by a hand, they joined Mum and Seth by the pond. Within minutes, they all headed back down the hill.

Back at the house, the girls kept their promise and showed Dad how much they had unpacked so far, mostly their toys and books. Rose had already made herself a display of her best and most special treasures, while Isabelle had neatly lined up her favourite books and pens on the little shelf next to her bed.

Once Dad had gone off to check how Seth was doing, they started whispering to each other. 'Can you believe it, Iz? Real fairies, *fairies*, and even more beautiful than I ever imagined them. We are so lucky!' Her deep blue eyes were shining with pure happiness as she hopped on and off her bed.

'I know! It's amazing. I wonder who else has met them.' Isabelle was a clever thinker and she wondered if any of the other children at school had ever seen the fairies. No one had mentioned it, but maybe it was too soon. 'I do hope we can keep them all to ourselves.'

'We need to tell Seth,' said Rose.

'I know, but not just yet,' said Isabelle. 'Dewdrop said that only children see *them*. I guess this means that there are lots more of them.'

Rose was delving into her favourite treasure box, pulling out each little gem or piece of shiny paper and making small piles. 'I'm looking for a gift for Dewdrop, to say thank you for the rose buds. We can give it to her tomorrow.'

'Yes, but tomorrow seems ages away.' Isabelle sat down on her bed with its new rabbit-covered duvet and picked up her favourite colouring book.

'I think I'm going to draw a picture of her so it doesn't all feel like a dream.' She started to draw Dewdrop, with her pale green dress and velvet slippers, her shimmering wings and her bouncy blonde curls. She sighed happily. 'She is quite lovely, isn't she? I can't wait to meet her friends.'

– CHAPTER FOUR –

Here Be Giants

The school day zoomed by, even though Isabelle could tell that Rose was restless and fidgety. Isabelle asked some of the girls in her class whether any of them lived near the park, but no one did, so she didn't ask anyone about the fairies. Part of her didn't want to share their secret anyway. *What is Dewdrop's home like?* she thought. *Maybe a treehouse or a little house hidden in the bushes.*

When she visited the school library, Rose looked in the local history section but couldn't see any books about fairy tales in Bristol. Perhaps only a few children had ever seen them, but no one had written it down. She did find lots of stories about love-struck giants and gem-filled grottoes though, so she borrowed a couple of books using her new library card.

Back at home Mum and Dad had almost finished unpacking and there were rows of empty boxes all along the hallway. Rose was torn between wanting to make dens out of them and wanting to see Dewdrop again, but in the end Mum made the decision for them.

'I'm sorry, girls, but I really want to get some more unpacking done. I can't do this if we go to the park. I promise you can go tomorrow.'

Mum ignored their sad faces as she unpacked a pile of heavy books onto the bookcase in the living room. Dad was crashing around in the cellar. His plan was to store equipment down there, until they could get some building work done. This was the main reason Mum and Dad had bought the house, as the vaulted cellar led out into a sweet little garden. There were three rooms leading back into the hillside. It got quite damp in the very back one, but Dad was planning to make it watertight, and turn the two front rooms into a new kitchen.

Mum and Dad were very excited about their plans and the girls were happy with their new bedroom, all painted and full of their things already. Seth had a good-sized room too, with a window looking out over the garden. They could hear him practicing on his guitar; he was pretty good.

Mum brought a few more boxes into their room. These contained even more books. Isabelle put them on the shelves, while Rose found her colouring pens and drew a door and windows on the biggest box. Once Isabelle had finished with the books, she drew tiny fairies on the box, each with a different colour dress and matching shoes. Then she found her favourite metallic pens and drew a tiny set of wings on each fairy. 'I wonder what all the other fairies look like,' she said. 'Do you think they will all look the same?'

Rose poked her head out of the box and examined Isabelle's pictures. 'I think they will all be very different and maybe there will be a king and queen fairy too!' She picked up a pencil and drew a king with a leaf crown and a queen with a tiara. She sat back to admire her work and then rubbed out the wings of the royal couple and drew them bigger. 'There, that's what I think.'

Isabelle added some extra jewels to the clothes with glitter glue and smiled at the result. 'Did you notice that Dewdrop's dress had tiny drops of water all over it? That's pretty magic. Why doesn't she get wet? Maybe it's her job to put the dewdrops out every morning.'

Rose smiled. 'Mummy always likes the Lady's Mantle leaves, remember. They collect little drops in the middle of the leaves and look really pretty. She said she thinks that the fairies drink from the leaves. Mummy believes in fairies, I'm sure she does. I wonder if she'd be able to see them.'

'Maybe,' Isabelle paused, 'but Dewdrop did

say adults can't and Mummy does worry a lot.'
They returned to silent colouring for a while,
each of the girls thinking about the fairies and
both looking forward to meeting more of them
soon.

After tea, which they ate sat on a rug in the
middle of the lounge because Dad hadn't found
the screws for the kitchen table yet, Rose helped
Dad and Seth put her doll's house together, while
Isabelle went back to their room with her new
library books.

She glanced through the one about the giants
first – Goram and Ghyston. They were brothers
and seemed pretty daft! Apparently they both
fell in love with a lady giant called Avalona, and
to win her heart they had to drain a lake for her.
They both started digging trenches from the lake;
Ghyston creating the gorge below the Clifton
Suspension Bridge and Goram digging a huge
trench near Blaise Castle. Isabelle remembered
Mum mentioning Blaise Castle. She read on...

Goram drank too much Somerset cider while he was digging and fell asleep. The brothers had been sharing an axe to dig and were throwing it back and forth to each other in turn. Silly Ghyston didn't check before throwing it to Goram, and because he was asleep Goram was killed by the axe. Isabelle rolled her eyes at this, but liked the story.

She discovered that Goram's body fell into the Avon and went down the river to the estuary where it formed the little islands Steep Holm and Flat Holm. She liked stories like this, where real things were explained by old stories and fairy tales. It made history much more fun! There was a little cave in the side of the gorge that Dad had pointed out when they walked across the bridge a few days previously. It was called the Giant's cave or Ghyston's cave and used to be the home of a hermit called St Vincent, so sometimes the giant Ghyston is called Vincent.

Isabelle put the book down and went to find Mum. She found her with her head inside a cupboard. She seemed to be cleaning.

'Mummy, did giants really exist?' asked Isabelle.

Mum's muffled voice said, 'Apparently, yes! Before we moved here I did a bit of research into the history of the city, and when the Trojans first arrived here on the island of Albion, which is what Great Britain used to be called, they found actual giant people, one was called Gogmagog! There's even a story of an Irish Giant who came to Bristol more recently, in the late seventeen hundreds, who was said to be more than 8ft tall!

'How tall am I, Mummy?' asked Isabelle.

'Well to put it simply, if you stood on Seth's shoulders, you'd be as high as the Irish Giant!'

'Did you know, Mummy, that the Avon Gorge was made by two silly giants who were fighting over a girl called Avalona? They named the river after her.'

Mum smiled. 'Wow, that's a good story. I'd like to hear more about that. Did you learn that from the library books you got at school?'

'Yes, and I got one about grottoes too. What's a grotto?'

Mum stood up and gave Isabelle a hug. 'Grottoes were fancy caves that men with too much money made on a whim just to impress their friends. They covered the walls of them with jewels and shiny shells, and often had sculptures made for them too, or used special lighting tricks. I guess they were supposed to just be a bit of fun really. There's one near here actually, just on the other hillside in Clifton Village, maybe we could go and have a look one day.'

Rose came dashing in and wanted Isabelle to come and see the doll's house. 'It looks amazing, Iz. It's a Georgian house, just like this one! It's got little furniture and everything, all tiny and so cute. Come and help me do the rooms. Dad and Seth have taken it to our bedroom.' Rose dashed off to their room where the new doll's house was now standing proudly between their two beds.

'Has it got a grotto?' asked Isabelle with a

cheeky smile.

'A whatto?!'

'It's a fancy cave, Mummy says, covered in jewels and shells. It sounds magical. She says there's one near here,' Isabelle whispered. 'Maybe we can ask Dewdrop about it tomorrow.'

'Good idea, I can't wait!'

fairies!'

– CHAPTER FIVE –
Towers and Tales

After school the following day, the girls quickly changed and waited for Mum eagerly. She was on the phone and Rose was making funny faces at her in a desperate attempt to get her to hurry up. Mum smiled into the phone and said goodbye. 'Okay, ready!'

Rose took a little bag with her that held the special gifts she'd made for Dewdrop: a tiny blanket that used to be held by an old cuddly toy, a green silk flower that she'd taken from her treasures box, and a piece of chocolate wrapped in foil. She was whispering urgently to Isabelle as they climbed up the hill towards the tower. 'Do you think fairies eat chocolate?'

Rose shrugged. 'I expect so, but I bet the chocolate they make is so much better than ours. I bet they make tiny sweets and decorate miniature fairy cakes with them. Oh, I'm so excited I can barely breathe!'

Halfway up the hillside, Mum sat down at the benches that looked out over the city. 'Off you go and explore then,' she said. 'I'll be right here. I've got some more calls to make and I can get better reception up here anyway! The trouble with having a lovely old house, with lovely old walls, is that they're so thick the signal can't get through!' She sat down at a free bench and was quickly distracted. Full of excitement, the girls raced off through the park to the hidden path.

'Dewdrop, are you there?' called Isabelle quietly into the bushes.

The air went still and there she was, skipping light as a feather towards them with a smile on her face. 'Oh, I'm so pleased to see you. I thought you'd forgotten me!'

Rose was always quick to be curious. She noticed Dewdrop was holding something shiny in each hand. 'We could never do that, but we're not allowed in the park on our own yet, so we had to wait for Mummy. What's that you've got?'

Dewdrop opened each hand and the girls saw she held a tiny golden key in each one. Both keys were the same and had an intricate carved set of wings in the loop at the top. In the centre of the wings was a single green gemstone, and the key hung from a thin golden chain.

'Each fairy has a set of keys they can give to just a few children at a time. I could tell from the very first time you came into the park that you were good children who would be able to keep our home secret, so these are for you. They unlock the door to the Fairy Hill.'

Both Rose and Isabelle took a sharp breath, their eyes as wide as the moon. They both took a key from her hands and placed the chain around their necks. Rose gazed at the tiny key, turning it over and over, and then holding it up to the light that filtered through the bushes. It sparkled like dew on the grass on a summer morning. 'Is that... an emerald?'

Dewdrop looked surprised. 'Wow, how did you know that?'

Isabelle giggled and held her own key up to the light too. 'My sister is a bit of a whiz when it comes to all things sparkly! Jewels, shiny paper, pearly buttons... anything that looks like treasure really. You should see the boxes she collects at home!'

'Oh, that reminds me,' said Rose with a laugh. 'I've brought you something to say thank you.' She opened up her little bag and pulled out the special gifts.

Dewdrop fluttered up to Rose's hand and landed gracefully on her palm. She picked up the tiny blanket and cuddled it close to her. 'Oh, that's so lovely and soft, thank you!' She wrapped it around her shoulders. She then picked up the silk flower, placed it expertly into her hair, and then popped the piece of chocolate into her mouth. 'Mmm, yummy! That's so very kind of you. It tastes of vanilla and honey, two of my favourite things!' Dewdrop twirled up into the air, her wings catching the light and casting rainbows around the girls. 'Do you have time to come and see where we live today?'

Rose and Isabelle looked at each other grinning. 'Yes, we do!'

'Then follow me.' Dewdrop flew out of the bushes and along the path, followed quickly by the twins. She headed up towards the tower standing tall on the hillside and glanced around to check they were still following her. As they walked Dewdrop told them about her home. 'Long, long, ago, there used to be a little shrine up here where sailors would pray to St Brendan the Navigator, to help them safely cross the seas from the harbour. The tower wasn't built until 1897 but we helped the architect, a Bristol man called William Venn Gough, to make it a beautiful tower, just like the other ones under the hill. You see, this is just the top of the real Fairy Hill, the rest of our home is hidden just under the hillside. Did you notice the angel on the top of the tower?' The girls nodded without speaking, not wanting Dewdrop to stop. 'Well, the city folk think that was put there to represent business or something, but actually we put it there, she's the Guardian of the Tower. She keeps an eye on everything that happens on the hill and around the park – she'll even let us know when your mum starts to worry about you. She warns us if there is any danger, which there has been several times over the centuries. She's seen all sorts of crazy things happen over the years: riots, plagues, wars, murders, but amazing things too, like the building of the Suspension Bridge, the SS Great Britain ship coming back into the docks, the first hot air balloons rising over Ashton Court (they're my favourite!). You see, the Fairy Hill has existed for a very long time, since the giants carved out the gorge and made the hills with all the soil.'

Isabelle gasped. 'Do you mean Goram and Ghyston? I've read about them, they fell in love with Avalona and made the Avon Gorge. Did they really make all the hills?'

They had reached the top of the hill and stepped into the tower.

'Yes, they did and there are lots of hidden entrances to the lands beneath if you look. Now, quickly, while there are no other people around. You have your keys?'

The girls both touched the tiny keys around their necks without speaking. 'Okay, so the secret entrance to our home is inside the tower. You see where the steps climb up?' The girls both nodded. 'Well, just to the side is the door.' Isabelle and Rose both stared at the wall, looking confused. Neither of them could see a door, just a blank wall. Dewdrop noticed that they were unsure. 'Trust me. Your keys will open the door. Isabelle, do you want to go first?' she asked.

Nodding enthusiastically Isabelle stepped forward to the wall and suddenly a golden keyhole appeared. She put the tiny key into the keyhole. It clicked as she turned it but this was no ordinary door – the wall simply vanished! In front of her she could see a set of stone steps. Stepping onto the first step it lit up in soft green and she was about to start following them down when Dewdrop stopped her.

'There's a much more fun way of going down quickly... sit down on the top step. This helps you get into the tower quickly so other people don't spot you.' Isabelle sat down obediently and the steps suddenly transformed into a slide. She laughed and pushed herself off.

Rose jumped back as the door suddenly reappeared in front of her again. 'Oh! Can't I go too?' She looked so disappointed.

Dewdrop giggled. 'Of course you can, but the door has to keep the secret you see, so it closes after each key turner. You have to use your key next.'

Rose quickly raised her key and giggled as the magical keyhole appeared again. Carefully turning her key, the wall disappeared and she sat down on the first step, which lit up a soft green once again, and pushed herself off. She squealed all the way down with happiness.

At the bottom of the slide she found herself in a light-filled cave. Isabelle was looking above her with her mouth wide open. Rose looked around; the walls were covered with a myriad of tiny shells and coloured jewels.

'It's a grotto!' breathed Isabelle.

Dewdrop smiled and led them out into the light. She spread her arms wide. 'Welcome to Fairy Hill!'

Under the Hill

As their eyes adjusted to the light, Rose and Isabelle gasped as a whole new world was opened up to them – a world full of clear light, blue skies, scented flowers and lush green grass. They were also no longer child-sized; they were as small as their new friend Dewdrop, although, as Rose quickly checked, they did not have tiny wings.

Stepping stone paths of pure white stones led them past pale stone homes with red-tiled roofs, each with a perfect garden filled with spring flowers. Fairies of every size and colour came excitedly out of their homes; stopped sweeping or picking early strawberries and flew to their gates to wave and smile at the new children. Dewdrop waved back at them. She turned to the girls.

'They're just as excited to see you, don't worry. We are all so happy when we find new children to love and be our friends. They are always very special.' She danced ahead beckoning the girls onwards.

Rose and Isabelle couldn't speak. They just kept grinning at each other and pointing at things they spotted. The path from the houses led into a courtyard that opened into a great sweep of trees, with stripy bunting fluttering between each tree and strings of fairy lights looping between them. Scrubbed wooden benches and tables were scattered under the trees and more fairies jumped up to come and say hello to the twins.

Two hawthorn trees at the edge of the circle were larger than the others and smothered in beautiful, pale pink flowers. Standing beneath them were two regal-looking fairies, a male wearing a crown made of green leaves and a female with majestic wings stretching out behind her. On her head she wore a

– CHAPTER SIX –

tiny crown of gold and silver jewels, with leaves twirling around each one, just like the pictures the girls had drawn at home on the packing boxes.

The Queen of Fairy Hill held out her hands to the girls. 'Welcome, Rose and Isabelle! Welcome to Fairy Hill and to our hearts. We are so pleased to meet you and hope you'll have many happy times with us.' The other fairies were standing quietly with joy on their faces. The air around the girls felt warm and filled with the scent of cherry blossom. 'It is a very special thing to be allowed to see our world. Dewdrop will be your trusted friend for the remainder of spring and then each of our season's fairies will be your guide through the year.'

Rose and Isabelle looked quizzically at Dewdrop. What did the queen mean? Dewdrop touched them gently on the arms and explained. 'There are fairies for each season. I am the Chief Fairy of spring. As the first summer blooms open and the swallows return, the spring fairies go to sleep, watched over by the Guardian of the Tower. The summer fairies, led by Sunburst, carry on the next season's work.

Leafbright wakes for autumn and Snowbell looks after winter. You see, it's very tiring looking after a season, so we sleep when it's not our turn.'

Rose frowned. 'But you must hardly ever see the other season's fairies?'

· Dewdrop smiled sadly at her. 'Well, actually we're seeing each other more and more but it's not necessarily a good thing. You see as the climate is changing we keep waking up in the wrong season. Then strange things happen because we're all out of sync. Last winter one of my spring fairies woke up too early and the Hill was suddenly covered in crocuses. The city folk loved it, but the poor flowers barely lasted a day.'

The king fluttered forward and bowed gently to the girls. 'It's a very great pleasure to welcome you, children. You will be safe here with us whenever you need help. Has Dewdrop mentioned that as soon as you step into our world time slows down a little?' The twins both shook their heads. 'So you can spend a little longer here with us without your family worrying. It's our little gift to you. As are these...' The King took a tiny silver wand from his pocket and tapped each of the girls gently on the head. The girls felt warmth spread through their bodies and a delicious tickling sensation on their backs. Turning they saw that they each now had a perfect pair of clear, shimmering wings. 'Dewdrop, why don't you give the girls a tour of Fairy Hill?'

Dewdrop bobbed over to the girls and did a little twirl, 'Shall we try out your wings? Think about them on your back. Your mind, heart and soul will all come together to lift you up.'

Isabelle was more confident and closed her eyes straight away, concentrating hard and quickly felt herself rising up. 'I'm flying!' She bobbed up and down a little, then tried a little twirl. 'Come on, Rose, it's wonderful!'

Rose watched Isabelle, looking a little worried. She scrunched her fingers into tight balls and bent her knees, like she was about to jump.

Dewdrop floated down beside her and touched her on the shoulder reassuringly, 'It's okay. Really it is. You can do this.' With a final little nod, Rose closed her eyes tightly and gracefully rose up into the air.

Isabelle flew over and said, 'Open your eyes, Rose, you're flying.'

Rose opened one eye, then the other and let out a heartfelt 'Ohhhhh!' She gave a little flutter of her wings, trying to turn and look at them, but each time chasing herself around in circles. Dewdrop and Isabelle giggled and each took one of Roses hands.

'Come and see our home,' said Dewdrop

She led them both through the trees and into a clearing where they saw a wide pool filled with green lily pads and tall blue irises. Fairies danced and spiralled in and out of the iris stems, chasing each other and laughing. A babbling stream led away from the pool, jumping over shiny pebbles where more fairies were dipping their feet in the cool water. They waved as the children passed by and a few of them came to say hello. 'I'm Suky. It's lovely to meet you. Do you want to come and play?' The twins checked with Dewdrop who said they could stay for a little while.

Rose carefully fluttered onto a rock and peered into the water. She could see silvery fish darting amongst the rocks and, as she leant a little closer, one of them jumped up and kissed her on the nose! She was so surprised she nearly fell into the water, but instead sat down with a plop and grinned at Isabelle who was laughing happily.

The next hour was the most magical of their lives as they listened to the tales of their fairy friends, sitting on the rocks by the stream. Every now and then new fairies would shyly wave at them or flutter past to take a peek at the new children. Dewdrop poured some dew from a tiny set of leaves into the bells of a lily-of-the-valley flower and passed them to the girls. It was delicious and the girls tried pouring some for themselves. Everywhere they looked they noticed little details in the flowers, the insects, the leaves. It felt as though their eyes could see better, stronger and with more light and colour than ever before.

A soothing voice was suddenly heard above them, or rather all around them; it felt like the sound passed through their bodies, like getting into a warm bath. They looked a little alarmed, but Dewdrop was quick to reassure, 'Don't worry, that's just the Guardian. She's letting you know it's time to go. Come on.' They fluttered back through the trees and past the waving fairies.

'When can we come again, Dewdrop?' asked Rose. Her big blue eyes looked so sad and Dewdrop stopped to give her a little hug.

'You can come as much as you like, and whenever you can.'

They had reached the Grotto at the foot of the tower by now and Isabelle had one last question, 'Where did all the beautiful shells come from? Do you have a beach under Fairy Hill?'

Dewdrop smiled. 'No, sadly no beach but we have other homes we can visit, all over the country, and over the centuries our family have collected precious things to protect them from being lost. We are a little like your museums where special things can be treasured. You see, not all fairy folk are good, some naughty dwarves stole some of our treasures and now we have pieces missing.' Dewdrop pointed to a small section of the grotto wall where there were deep holes amongst the shells and jewels. 'The Grizzles, that's what we call the bad dwarves, they stole these. We don't know where they are.'

Isabelle gasped, 'Maybe we could help you find them?' Isabelle's eyes were sparkling with excitement. She loved a mystery.

Dewdrop had her head on one side, thinking. 'Perhaps you could. We heard that the Grizzles hadn't gone far before they lost them. They stole one spiny shell and two beautiful gems, but when they took them above ground they returned to their normal size. The silly Grizzles couldn't carry them far. They aren't very clever!'

Isabelle jumped up and down, her wings sparkling even more brightly with her excitement. Rose watched thoughtfully. She thought about her wings and wondered what else they could do. She tried to concentrate hard and think about blue skies. She opened her eyes, turned slowly to catch a glimpse of her wings and was delighted to see them tinged with blue. Next she tried picturing thousands of flowers and when she looked, her wings were indeed covered with petals.

Dewdrop was impressed. 'Well done, Rose, you've discovered the magic of wing-change already! It's how we show how we are feeling and it's also how we are able to disappear so quickly if an adult tries to see us – we can make ourselves camouflaged.' Dewdrop turned back to Isabelle. 'You could ask some of our friends around the city. They might know something that would lead to our missing treasures. You could try the keeper of the Goldney Grotto first.'

Isabelle nodded quickly, already thinking of a plan. 'How will we know your friends?'

'Don't worry, you'll see, but for now it's time for you to return. Your mother has finished her calls in the park, but remember time has ticked more slowly while you were here, so she won't be worried.'

Rose stood at the bottom of the slide looking up. She was frowning. 'How do we get up?' Dewdrop tapped the slide with her little green wand and the slide became stone steps, with a twisting, golden handrail leading them back to the surface. Each step lit up as they walked, guiding them all the way to the top. Dewdrop gave them a quick squeeze, before each of them stepped through the magical doorway back into the tower entrance. As they glanced behind, they heard her call softly through the closed door. 'Goodbye till next time!' The sisters gave each other a big hug and ran back down to find Mum, who was happy to see them come back so quickly as though no time had passed at all.

CHAPTER SEVEN

The Grotto Diamonds

The next day was Saturday and a gloriously sunny weekend stretched before the three children. At breakfast Mum told them that she'd seen a poster saying the Goldney Gardens were going to be open to the public that day, and would they like to go and see the grotto. Isabelle and Rose couldn't believe their luck and Seth wondered why they were so excited.

'What's the big deal with the grotto, girls?' he asked them, while they finished off their breakfast. The twins looked at each other and nodded. They both knew what the other was thinking – it was time to share their secret with Seth. After all, they might need his help.

Isabelle took a deep breath. 'Seth, we have a secret to tell you, but you must promise not to tell anyone else, nobody at all.' She looked at him gravely.

Rose held out her little finger to Seth, 'You have to pinky promise!'

'Okay!' said Seth, taking Roses little finger with his own and shaking it up and down. 'I pinky promise! Now what's the big secret?'

Isabelle and Rose took it in turns to quickly tell their brother everything that had happened so far. Seth didn't say a word, just kept looking from one sister to the next, trying to decide if this was another of their elaborate stories or for real. It was an incredible story and he wasn't sure he believed it, but he decided to play along. Eventually he got a chance to speak, 'If the tower does go further down under the ground, and there is a land of fairies under Brandon Hill, what about all the other hills?'

'Well, that's the thing,' replied Rose. 'Dewdrop

says the hills were made by the giants when they carved out the Avon Gorge and the one by Blaise Castle. She said that there are lots of hidden doors into the hills. Have you seen any?'

Seth paused for a moment. Maybe they were telling the truth. 'Actually now I think about it, I have! On my walk to school and when we've walked around Clifton Village. There are even some on St Michael's Hill too. I just presumed they were cellars or something.' All three children were silent for a while as they thought of the endless possibilities of what could be found under the hills of Bristol.

They decided they would all keep their eyes peeled when they walked to Goldney Hall Gardens and try to spot some more doors.

The walk from Brandon Hill to Clifton was up and down hills too. The children spotted several mysterious passageways and blocked archways on the way. Now that they had it in their thoughts they seemed to see so much clearer. Mum was delighted that everyone seemed to be enjoying their trip out so much. She'd not seen Seth quite so eager to explore for a while and was hoping that this meant he was feeling more settled. When they arrived at the little door in the hillside leading into the Gardens, a friendly lady with a strong Bristolian accent, smiled thoughtfully down at them as she gave them a map of the gardens. She explained that they would be best to head straight to the Grotto as it would get busy later. The children checked the map to find the grotto. As they walked across the lawn, in front of the pretty orangery, Rose spotted a small tower and ran ahead. Isabelle and Seth glanced at each other and then ran to catch up.

'Do you think it's another secret entrance, Seth?' Isabelle was very happy to be able to talk to her big brother about the secret at last.

'Maybe? Look, there's a sign here. It says the tower has a steam engine that powers the water fountain in the grotto.'

'Let's go and find the grotto. I can see a little

door down that path over there.' Rose ran off again and the others quickly followed. There were a few visitors milling around by the pond and some drinking cups of tea outside the orangery, but other than that the gardens were quiet so the children knew they had their chance. They'd left Mum back at the steam engine tower talking to one of the guides, but they didn't have long. They dashed down the steps, through the gothic-arched doorway and then froze as they stared around them. The cave was covered on every surface with shells, strange shapes and lots of glittering stones. They could hear water and found a small fountain running from a statue deep in a crevice. They could see a lion made of stone and, hiding behind him, a lioness in another cave.

'Wow!' said Seth, and the girls just nodded in awe. It was a truly amazing sight.

Rose examined the sparkling stones and Isabelle tried to get a better look at the ceiling when suddenly, they heard a deep voice behind them.

'Welcome, children of Fairy Hill!'

They all turned in surprise and saw the statue at the top of the fountain looking straight at them and glowing brightly. Seth smiled. Of course, his sisters had been telling the truth, and this proved it.

Rose was the first to speak, taking it in her stride that it was completely normal for the statue to be talking to them. 'Hello, I'm Rose and this is Isabelle and Seth. What's your name, are you a god?'

'Indeed I am. A river god, Neptune, if you will. It's an honour to meet you all.'

Isabelle moved closer to the statue. 'Hello, this is a lovely grotto. I wonder if you can tell us a bit more about how all these stones got here please?' She liked to get straight to the point and knew they only had a little time. 'And do you talk to everyone?'

The river god laughed a deep gurgling laugh. 'Oh no, not everyone. Only special children. You see, I can feel the magic in you, and I can tell that you have met the fairies of Fairy Hill.'

Seth noticed he didn't move much as he talked; just his face seemed to crease more like real skin. Seth had a sudden thought and turned to look at the two lions behind them, who were now yawning and nuzzling each other gently.

'Iz, Rose, look!'

The girls turned to see what Seth had spotted. They were a little scared at first, but Rose moved slowly towards the lions and as they watched her, she reached out and stroked the stone fur. The male lion purred loudly and went back to licking his mate.

The river god spoke again, 'Don't worry, no magical creature will hurt you. In fact you'll meet lots more of our friends around the city. Be careful of the gargoyles though, they can be a bit tricksy...' Seth couldn't believe what he was hearing, remembering that he'd been joking with his sisters the other day about statues coming to life.

The river god continued, 'The grotto was made by a man called Thomas Goldney a long time ago, around 1739. There was a lot of activity in Bristol at the time; buildings springing up all over the place, lots of money being exchanged and lots of fabulous parties! Goldney made this grotto to show off to his friends, but he certainly did a good job. I particularly love the Bristol diamonds.'

At the mention of gems, Rose's full attention came back from stroking the lions to the god, 'Diamonds! Real ones?'

'Well no, not real in the usual sense, but when those silly giants, Goram and Ghyston, were digging out the gorge, they found huge quantities of these quartz stones, and they became known as Bristol diamonds.'

Isabelle, looking thoughtful, asked, 'Have any of your stones been stolen recently?' She was thinking of the missing treasures in the Fairy Hill grotto.

'Well, actually we did have some of those awful Grizzles try and steal some not long ago. I could hear Hercules up there trying to get rid of them.'

'Who's Hercules?' asked Rose curiously.

'He's my old buddy up there by the tower. Don't get to talk to him much. We have to yell to each other when there's no one around, you see. Anyway those greedy dwarves were making a lot of fuss and nonsense about something, and it sounded like they were carrying something heavy. Next thing I knew, there was a lot of crashing and a huge gem came bouncing down into the grotto. Not much I could do about it, but the next day the gardener just presumed it had fallen off somewhere and added it to the display. It's over there in the corner, look.' He nodded to a corner of the grotto. Seth and Rose followed his gaze and found a particularly sparkly stone set in the wall, different to the others around it.

Rose touched it carefully, running her small fingers over the purply, glass-like edges. 'We think it was stolen from the Fairy Hill grotto.

The river god frowned. 'Oh dear! I knew those Grizzles were up to no good! Pesky little creatures they are.'

'Can we take it back to the fairies please?'

asked Isabelle.

The river god took a deep breath. 'My dearest children, all you need to do is touch your fairy key, make a wish and the gem will be returned to its rightful place.'

The twins closed their eyes (because that's what you do under such circumstances) and wished. Seth crossed his fingers and wished too. The sparkly stone faded away, leaving an empty space where it had once been.

The two stone lions stopped licking each other for a while and seemed to nod at the children for completing their task.

Suddenly they heard footsteps coming down the steps. It was Mum. 'There you are. Wow, this is quite something, isn't it? What beautiful lions, they almost look real!' The children giggled but all the statues had frozen once more. The children showed Mum around the rest of the cave, pointing out their new friend the river god, and then she headed back out of the grotto saying, 'Time for tea and cake, I think.'

The children all cheered and started to head up the steps but they heard a voice behind them quietly say, 'Do say hello to old Hercules up there for me as you go! Tell him to use that bat of his to see off those dwarves next time!'

They turned back to the river god and waved, nodding that they would.

They found Hercules up on the lawn as he had said, a large statue holding a club of some sort, ready to swing at an unseen pest. Rose went up close to his head and whispered the message to him from his friend. She was delighted when he winked at her. She joined the others and they all went to find Mum at the orangery, ready for cakes to celebrate their discovery of one of the stolen gems.

CHAPTER EIGHT

Picnic With a Chicken!

It was Sunday. Everyone in the house with the yellow door enjoyed a long breakfast sitting out in the little sunny back garden. Mum was pottering around poking at plants and snipping dead flowers off their stalks contentedly. Dad was already at work pulling bits of old wood out of a store shed, and making a pile by the garden gate ready to take to the dump. Seth was helping him, at the same time telling Dad all about his new school friends. The girls had tidied away the breakfast things, and then found their box of Fairy House pieces.

'You can use that little corner of the garden if you like,' said Mum, pointing to a patch of daisies that was growing at the bottom of the steps. 'It would make a lovely fairy garden.'

Rose and Isabelle happily spent most of the morning creating miniature fairy homes amongst the daisies, adding the little animals and tiny fairy figures they'd had for their last birthday from Grandma. There were replica gates, tiny logs, mushrooms, ladybirds, a fairy-sized lamppost and little white mice. Two pure white unicorns stood proudly in the centre, and each had a fairy with blue wings standing next to them. On her way back into the house carrying some cut flowers, Mum came over to inspect their handiwork. She told them that Grandma would like to see what they had made when she came to stay in a few week's time. The girls couldn't wait. Grandma was always so much fun to have around because she believed all their stories. She even told them her own magical stories.

'Grandma has seen a fairy you know, Iz,' said Rose. 'Remember she told us about it?' Rose moved one of the unicorns slightly to the left and sat back on her heels to admire her work.

'Yes, I remember,' said Isabelle. 'It was quite a sad

story though, wasn't it? She wasn't feeling well and saw a fairy sitting by her bedroom window on a plant pot. I used to be so jealous that she had seen one. Imagine what she's going to say when we tell her about our fairies!'

Isabelle nodded and carefully picked up her fairy figure. Gazing at it she said, 'I wonder if all fairies are the same; if our fairies are like the one Grandma saw. That would make her really happy if she could see one again.'

Rose looked thoughtful for a moment before she replied, 'But I don't think she can see them anymore. She's never told us she's seen any since she was a little girl. Maybe the magic has gone for her too.'

Isabelle looked sad. 'I hope the magic never goes. I want to see fairies forever and ever and ever.' She placed the fairy carefully back with the unicorns again.

Mum called down from the kitchen and asked if they wanted to have a picnic on College Green at lunchtime. 'We could go for a walk afterwards maybe?'

Seth appeared at his bedroom window and winked at the girls. 'We could get a better look at those golden unicorn *statues*, girls, couldn't we?' he said.

At first the twins didn't understand what he meant and why he was winking at them, but it suddenly dawned on them, both at the same 'twin-time' and they nodded vigorously.

'Great idea, yes please, Mummy.'

They put the fairy things back into the box and took them to the storeroom before going to help Mum make the picnic. Rose loved helping make special food for everyone. Finger food was her speciality!

Isabelle headed to Seth's room, knocking firmly on his door as he had instructed. 'You may enter,' he said with a deep wise voice.

Isabelle giggled and pushed the door open. She plopped down on the bed and frowned at Seth. 'So, what are you thinking? How can the unicorns help? They're right up on top of the Council Office, aren't they? We can't talk to them up there.'

Seth spun his chair round to face his curious sister. 'I'm not exactly sure yet, but it will come to me once we get down there. Have no fear, small one. Your brother has a plan... sort of.'

It was a lovely warm spring day and the birds were singing as the whole family walked down the hill towards College Green, which stood between their new school, the Cathedral and City Hall. All three children were squinting up at the golden unicorns high on the two ends of the curved brick building, wondering how on earth they would be able to talk to them.

'Why all the squinting?' asked Dad, looking up and trying to see what had caught their attention. He wasn't used to his three chatty children being so quiet. He was usually trying to get a word in amongst their nattering.

'Just looking at those pretty unicorns, Daddy,' said Isabelle. 'They're so golden in the sunshine.'

Mum had found a good spot on the grass near some other families. Rose was laying out the different boxes of food that she and Mum had prepared. 'There's salami and olives and some yummy French stick, Daddy's pickles and Mummy's caperberries, and our favourite pâté. Did we bring knives?'

Mum took the cutlery out and Dad poured some lemonade, before settling back to watch them all tuck in. It made him happy to take some time out with his family in his home city. He was proud of how well they'd all settled in already, and he was looking forward to showing them more of his childhood home.

Lunch done, Mum and Dad lay back on the grass enjoying the sunshine on their faces while the children ran over towards the City Hall.

They all looked up at the golden statues thinking. Seth had an idea. 'I've got it! Look at the old chapel. There's a golden cockerel. Maybe we could ask him to fly over and talk to the unicorns for us?' He found a spot where there were less people. 'Girls, over here,' he shouted. Rose and Isabelle joined him, looking up at the little golden chicken.

'How do we get him to talk to us?' asked Isabelle.

Suddenly there was a fluttering of wings and next to them stood the golden cockerel. The children couldn't believe their eyes! Seth looked around anxiously, wondering why nobody had noticed a golden bird flying down to the Green.

'Don't you worry, my lad, busy folks rarely see what's going on in front of them. See? Nobody looking. All too busy.' The cockerel bounced around them, wiggling his legs in the air and rolling his big eyes, but no one even glanced their way. 'We live in a similar time-realm to the fairy-folk you see.'

The twins were spellbound, neither of them speaking. Rose was the first to talk. 'Hello, sir. Can I call you, sir?'

The cockerel pulled himself up even taller and puffed his chest out proudly. 'You, young lady, may call me whatever you like, but Frank's the name. Happy to meet those with the fairy touch. You must be the new children of Fairy Hill?'

They all looked surprised.

'Thought so. News travels fast round the hills of Bristol, you know. What can I help you with? I'm at your service.' He sat down on the ground, tucking his wings in neatly. The children sat down around him. Anyone walking by would have taken him for a toy bird, he sat so very still.

'My name's Seth. We're searching for missing jewels and shells from the grotto inside Fairy Hill. Do you know anything about it? Or do you think the unicorns might know?'

Frank cocked his golden head to one side and glanced warily up at the unicorns. 'Mmm, I can't say I've heard anything, although those Grizzles are always up to something – crazy bunch. As for the unicorns, let me fly on up there and ask them, although they can be a bit hoity-toity. It's because they live higher than the rest of us, especially that Gerald...' He rolled his eyes and fluffed himself out again. 'Jemima is just plain nosey, but that might help us in this case. Back in a bit,' he said, and off he flew.

The children could see him glinting in the sunlight on the roof. Every now and then a unicorn appeared to move its head and paw at the ground gently. All three children wished they could fly up there too.

A few minutes later, Frank dropped back down next to them, as gracefully as a chicken could possibly manage.

'As I thought, Jemima has eyes and ears all over the

city. Bristol must have at least one statue of every creature on the planet I reckon, from the iguana on Whiteladies Road, to those poor little dogs stuck swimming in Millennium Square; they get ever so tired you know, those poor little terriers!'

Rose couldn't believe it. 'Do you mean to say that every single statue in Bristol can come alive?'

Frank cocked his head on one side once again. 'Pretty much, yes. Although some choose not to bother. Keep themselves to themselves, they do. Anyway, Jemima says you should ask the fox at the top of the hill. On the corner of the building that looks Italian with arched windows and doors. He's a wily old thing, and has a pretty good view of all that's going on. Fred's his name.' Frank started to rise up on his big golden wings. 'I'd best go. Your parents are coming. Good luck!'

The sun was so bright that Mum was shielding her eyes. 'What was that? I'm sure I saw a chicken flying away. It must have been a pigeon in the sunlight.' The children giggled. 'Ready to head up Park Street?' she asked.

THE BRISTOL DINOSAUR
THECODONTOSAURUS

CHAPTER NINE

A Trail of Statues

They all followed Mum and Dad along the grass to Park Street, a steep hill lined with vintage clothes shops and bars, filled with laughing students relaxing on their time off. Halfway up the hill Isabelle suddenly stopped and pointed at a black and white sign above a shop. 'Look, Mum, Goram and Vincent, that's the two giants I was telling you about. The ones that dug the Avon Gorge and made the Bristol Hills! I wonder what the sign's there for?'

Mum looked up at the building, spotting the large letters G & V in the window. Dad already had his phone out and was looking it up. 'Ah, sadly not a giant's lair. It's an advertising company. They must have heard of the story too, good choice for a name. It got your attention! Maybe I'll see if they need any photographers...' Dad continued up the hill, looking deep in thought. Seth looked at him sympathetically. Dad was always worrying and it made him sad sometimes. He wished he was a bit older and could do more to help. Maybe get a paper-round or something.

'Have you spotted any foxes yet?' asked Rose at Seth's shoulder.

He shook his head. 'No, but we're not at the top yet.'

They continued up the hill, looking around them all the time, while Mum and Dad were chatting quietly to each other. They reached the double traffic lights at the top and, as they stood waiting for the lights to change, Isabelle suddenly cried out, 'Fox!'

The others all jumped and looked where she was pointing, while Mum and Dad wondered why on earth an urban fox would be out in the city at this time of day. They'd seen plenty of them around the area at night, but this was the middle of one of the busiest pedestrian and traffic zones of the city.

Dad looked quizzically at Isabelle. 'Where's the fox,

Iz?'

Isabelle tried to be less excited. 'Oh, it's just a fox statue over on that building, the one with all the *arched windows and doors.*' She emphasised the last few words to make clear to Seth and Rose what she meant. She had actually found the fox the unicorn had mentioned!

Seth was first to understand. 'That's a lovely old building, Mum. Can we go and get a better look?' Mum and Dad glanced at each other, surprised at their eldest son's sudden need to examine buildings. They shrugged and crossed over to the square building with its Venetian arches and olive trees on the veranda.

Dad smiled at Mum. 'Looks like a good spot for an ice cream, don't you think, Mum?'

Mum grinned and nodded. 'Yes, please. That was quite a hill climb after all. I think we could all do with something cold.' Dad ushered them up the steps and found a table with a parasol. Then he headed inside to order.

Rose was practically bouncing up and down on her chair. 'Mummy, can we go and have a look at the fox Iz spotted please? It's just around the corner.' Mum nodded and settled back in the shade of the parasol, enjoying the buzz of the city.

The children dashed down the steps and around the corner of the building. All along the wall were other creatures, who all turned to stare as they felt the fairy-touched children nearby.

The fox looked at them, a bored expression on his pointy features. 'Yessss?' he said slowly, with a slightly Italian drawl.

Rose was trying not to laugh. 'Helloooo,' she said, in the same tone as the fox.

The fox looked at her crossly for a moment, but then smiled and chuckled. 'So, fairy-children, what are you up to this fine spring afternoon?'

Seth decided he should try his best Queen's English on the fox. 'Kind gentleman, you are obviously a respectable fellow of this grand city, and we wondered whether you might have seen or heard of any Grizzles in the area. Maybe trying to carry something far too big for them?'

Isabelle was looking at Seth as though he'd gone slightly mad. Instead she tried the more direct approach. 'We are helping the fairies of Brandon Hill find some missing jewels and shells from their grotto. The unicorns on City Hall said you might be able to help. Sir, please.'

Fred the fox paused and looked at them, one at a time, painfully slowly. The children all held their breath in anticipation.

Rose was first to crack, letting out a huge sigh and flinging her hands in the air dramatically. The fox rolled his eyes and smiled. 'Patience, dear child. It's good to stop and think occasionally. You should try it.' He paused while she considered this. 'Now I think about it, there was quite a kerfuffle around here a few months back, and usually kerfuffle's are caused by Grizzles. This lot seemed to be trying to carry something across from the hill. I think they were heading towards the Downs; they kept dropping things and trying to pick them up again, but making a right bungle of the whole thing. They gave up after a while and left something down by the museum. The curator was very excited when he arrived the next morning, whooping and displaying all sorts of un-gentlemanly behaviour at something he'd found, so I guess that might have been something to do with it?'

None of the children spoke. They were all looking quickly from one to the other, nodding happily. 'Do you know what he did with whatever he found?' asked Rose.

Fred twitched his nose and said, 'Well I suppose he took it into the museum with him. That's what I would have done.'

Rose and Isabelle hugged each other, thanked the fox, and ran back to see Mum. They were just in time as Dad had arrived with the ice creams. Seth stayed to thank the fox, but to his disappointment found that as soon as the girls left, with all their inner fairy-touched magic, the fox turned back to stone again. Seth left feeling a little sad.

Back on the terrace, the girls were feasting on ice creams, getting in their usual mess. Dad was rolling his eyes at them, but it was obvious that nothing could spoil his mood today. It was just so lovely to be out and about. 'Where next then, kids, the museum maybe?' he asked with a smile, thinking he was making a joke. His children were not huge fans of looking at old relics, preferring to be playing outside whenever they could.

'Yes, definitely,' said Isabelle enthusiastically. To Mum and Dad's surprise they were up and off down the steps toward the museum before either of them could comment. They quickly followed, looking at each other in amazement.

'Our children are full of surprises,' said Mum.

'Indeed,' said Dad.

Whispering quickly to each other as they went through the entrance foyer of the grand museum and up the marble stairs, Isabelle made a plan. 'If the Grizzles dropped either a shell or a jewel outside then we need to find the geology section, I think.' They entered through heavy wooden doors with shiny brass doorknobs and gazed upwards as they found themselves in a large open room where a huge plane was hanging from the ceiling.

Dad, who had caught up with them, explained over their shoulders, 'That's a Bristol Boxkite. Quite a beauty, isn't she?'

They nodded and Rose quickly asked, 'Daddy, do you know if there is a shell or gems section here? I'd really like to see some jewels.'

'Yes, it's upstairs, I think. I seem to remember there being fossils and all sorts up there. Why don't you all go and have a wander, and we'll meet you back here in twenty minutes. Seth's got a watch on. I want to show Mummy the old maps of Bristol.'

The children sped off up the stairs, with Rose enjoying the curly, golden handrails that led all the way up to the top. On the first floor they came face-to-face with the Bristol dinosaur, Theco, who was found on the Downs in 1834. As they stood admiring him, Rose felt the hairs on the back of her neck rise and could sense someone watching them. She turned quickly, just in time to see a very tall man disappear around the corner. She frowned and followed the others to a gorgeous painted Gypsy caravan that they all thought would be a wonderful place to live. They met Alfred the Gorilla, a huge stuffed creature that used to live at Bristol Zoo and were fascinated by all the different stuffed animals in glass cases, although Rose got quite upset at the thought of them all being dead. Seth was trying his best to explain how it was important to be able to study the animals, when Rose caught sight of the same tall man again, this time looking at them through the glass from the end of the room. She decided to be brave and headed straight for him, but when they reached the end of the room he had vanished again.

Finally they came to the geology room. There was case after case of fossils and more brightly lit cupboards full of sparkly gems of all colours and sizes, but Isabelle spotted a case standing all by itself and called the others over to look. 'This one. It has to be this one, look "The Bristol Diamonds"! They look just like the ones from the Fairy Hill grotto. And look it says, "These specimens were found during the development of Clifton in the nineteenth century." These, I reckon, are the missing jewels!'

The children all stared into the case, noses pressing against the glass. Suddenly a booming voice said, 'Excuse me, do you mind standing a little further back from the case please? We wouldn't want it falling on you, would we?' The tall imposing-looking man in a dark suit was peering down at them gravely. 'Nice to see you're so interested in these gems I must admit. Found one of them myself actually only recently. It was just outside the museum. Very odd to be honest, but I'm not one to turn a gift-horse down!'

Rose was practically bouncing up and down. 'It's true, it's true. We've found them!'

The man frowned at her. 'Found what, I just said I found this latest one.' He appeared to scowl at Rose. 'But if you want to take some of your own gems home, there's a lovely shop downstairs.' He gave them a thin-lipped smile, shooed them away, and whipped out a duster to give the glass case a wipe. 'All very well having children interested,' he said quietly, 'but why do they have to *touch* everything.

The children ran down the staircase until they were out of sight of the scary man.

'There's no way we will be able to get those gems,' Isabelle said with a sigh.

'We will just have to tell the fairies where we found them, and hopefully they will be able to get them all back themselves. At least we got them the one from the grotto,' Rose responded.

Mum and Dad were waiting for them. The children pleaded for a quick look in the shop before they went, and were rewarded with a £1 coin each to spend. After a quick look around at the pencils and mugs with artwork on them, they soon found a table filled with wooden compartments selling shiny marbles, boxes of tiny fossils, and just the thing they were seeking – gems. There were all sorts of crooked and smooth ones, of all sizes and colours, but they each picked one and took them up to the counter. The assistant smiled at them all. 'Oooh, what lovely jewels, like treasure they are, just like the Bristol Diamonds themselves. You know, they used to be made into cheap jewellery. I remember my grannie having some. You look after them mind.'

Putting the new treasure in their pockets the children went back to Mum and Dad and headed back into the sunshine. As they left the building Rose glanced back. She saw the tall man stood at the top of the steps, hands behind his back, nose in the air watching them leave.

– CHAPTER TEN –

The Final Piece of the Puzzle

'So, where next?' asked Mum. Seth, Rose and Isabelle all looked at each other and shrugged. They'd found the grotto gem and the museum gem, but they had no idea where the shell might be.

'Are there any shell sculptures anywhere, Dad?' asked Seth.

Dad laughed and looked puzzled. 'Why do you need to find shells?'

Seth paused and wasn't sure what to say, but Isabelle came to his rescue. 'We're playing a sort of game, Daddy, where we find a sculpture of every letter in the alphabet. We've seen unicorns, and a cockerel, and a fox. Now we want to see if there are any shells.' It was a dubious answer and they could tell Mum and Dad were a bit confused, but Rose distracted them by pointing across the road to where she'd spotted the tower on Brandon Hill, peeping out from behind the trees. She wasn't expecting to see it from here, so they must be walking around the hillside. 'Can we please go back through the park to get home? There's the tower so we can't be far away.'

Dad suggested they could go back via the other side of the hill, but on the way he wanted to show them one last old building. The children groaned a bit, but at least they would be able to go through the park again, and maybe they'd have time to see Dewdrop.

At the end of a row of shops, the road opened up around a triangle of green, where a soldier stood in metal holding his rifle in front of him. Seth saw him glance their way but it was far too busy to talk to him, especially as he was standing in the middle of two busy roads. Dad pointed just behind and said, 'That's the Vic Rooms. I think the university uses it for teaching music now. If we cross over we can head back down the hill and go home via the park.'

On each side of the steps stood a magnificent lion, their heads held proud above their huge bronze paws. With a nod to the girls, Seth took Mum and Dad over to the fountain and started asking questions about the figures there, while Rose and Isabelle quickly ran over to one of the lions.

'Hello, young fairy-friends, my name's Rufus. What a fine day for enjoying this glorious city. How can I help?'

The children were used to talking statues by now. They quickly introduced themselves and explained their quest for the lost shell.

'Oh, that's an easy one!' Rufus said, shaking out his mane just a little. Rose looked over at Mum and Dad to see if they could see, but Seth had them turned facing the other way. 'You see,' he continued in a deep, slow voice. 'It's right here, or rather, right there, in the fountain. I enjoyed scaring those dreadful Grizzles away that night. Made them jump so far they dropped the shell where dear Triton (he's a Greek God you know, messenger of the sea), quickly made it part of the fountain. It's the spiny shell in the front. The mermaids weren't particularly pleased about the addition, mind you. Gave them less room for lounging about combing their hair.' Rufus rolled his eyes and yawned. The girls quickly thanked him and ran back to the fountain, where Seth was pointing out various creatures. 'Look, girls there are so many different ones when you really look. There's a seal and an octopus of all things!' He raised a questioning eyebrow at them, wondering if they'd found out anything from the lion.

Isabelle nodded rapidly at him, and then pointed at the shell lying in front of the fountain, 'And look at that gorgeous, *very unusual* shell, Seth!'

Seth understood at once and let out a big laugh. 'Wow, what a day it's been for discoveries!'

Mum smiled at him. 'You're right, Seth, I'm exhausted. Let's head home. Lead the way, Dad!'

Worn out from their successful mission, the children were happy to be heading back home. The sun was getting lower in the sky and the city breathed a sigh of relief that another busy day was coming to an end. Dad led them up some steep steps, using up the very last of their energy, but when they arrived at the top they were surprised to find themselves behind the tower at the top of Brandon Hill.

They sat down on a bench for a while to catch their breath and all enjoyed watching the grey squirrels gambling around them, falling over each other in play and shooting up and down the tree trunks. They seemed very tame and Rose desperately tried to get one of them to come to her hand. She made a note to herself that next time they should bring some nuts to feed them.

Seth wandered over to the tower with Isabelle and she showed him where the magic door was. Rose ran over. 'Quick, Mum and Dad have said we can stay up here for a bit. They're going to walk home now and said not to be long. Let's go and tell Dewdrop about our finds!'

Seth looked sad, 'It's a shame I can't come with you. I'd love to see what's down there.'

He pictured everything they had told him about,

the grotto, the little houses, the orchard and the king and queen. It all sounded magical. Seth watched open-mouthed as they used their keys and disappeared through the magic door, down into Fairy Hill. He stood guard by the tower, but it seemed like only a few minutes had passed before they were back again. 'Gosh, that was quick, you were only gone a few minutes! What happened?'

Rose giggled, 'Remember how we told you time slows down when we're with the fairies? We've been gone for an hour but to you it was no time at all!'

Between them the girls told Seth what had happened, how Dewdrop was there to meet them at the bottom of the slide and how she took them straight to see the king and queen with their news. 'They were so happy, Seth, to get the grotto gem back. And they now know where the rest are. But even better than that, they gave us this, for you.' Isabelle held out her hand. It was a tiny golden key on a thin woven chain, just like the girls'. Seth looked from one twin to the next, who were both grinning from ear to ear like they'd won the best prize.

'When the king and queen found out what you had done to help us find the missing treasures, they decided to make you part of Fairy Hill too. This key is for you!'

Seth couldn't speak, he was dumbstruck. He took the tiny key from his little sister's hand and grinned. 'Let's go then!'

Rose put her hand on his arm quickly, 'Hold on, there's one other thing they said when they gave us your key.'

Seth paused and looked quizzically at his sister, 'Okay, what is it?'

Rose took a deep breath, feeling very important and continued, 'They told us there have been strange things happening down at the harbour – things that might put Fairy Hill at risk and they'd like our help.'

Seth grinned, ready for his next adventure. He put the key around his neck, then stood in front of the door and gasped when a keyhole appeared. Turning the key in the tiny lock the door disappeared once more, showing the tunnel and the stone steps. With a deep, happy breath he sat down as they'd told him, and laughed out loud all the way to the bottom. It was the best feeling in the world.

He found himself in the grotto and was quickly joined by his squealing sisters. He stepped out into the light of Fairy Hill, tiny as a mouse! He gazed in wonder all around him. This was the start of a whole new world of adventure for Seth, Isabelle and Rose.

THE END

Join the children in book two – where we meet the Summer Fairy, Sunburst, and have lots of fun and daring adventures by the harbour.

THANK YOU

Granfer / Dad (for never, ever doubting my
ambitions and crazy ideas!)
Granma / Mum (who still believes)
Marie Suzanne Hallworth
Stephanie Jane Owen
Joseph David Hallworth
Oliver Mark Hallworth
Ashleigh Jane Blake
Amelia Grace Owen
Harry Jon Foord Owen
Georgina Knapp
Jasmine Nava
Hazel Nava
Mia Grace Richardson
Emily Marie Stahl-Timmins

Thank you all for believing

x

#fairytaleofbristolbook
@fairytaleofbristolbook